ERIC HOOVER

LOVE ME TO DEATH

VOL.1

A MURDER BY MISTAKE

TABLE OF CONTENT

INTRODUCTION

Logan and Oliver were best of friends, Oliver became infatuated over Jane a girlfriend to Logan. Jane didn't want to have anything to do with Oliver so she consistently rejected him. Oliver grew jealous of the romantic affairs between the two lovers and as such, he plotted to poison Jane to death in a juicy drinks unfortunately Logan drank the poison and died. Investigation was sure to take place but would they find the killer?

CHAPTER ONE

FAMILY FRIENDSHIP

It was 10:15am. Frank, a giant man in his early 60's, his balding head and bold eyes make him look more aggressive than he is in the real sense. He stood knocking on the door.

Felicia, an eight years old girl with curling hair and tiny voice answered. "Yeah who is there?"

Frank "it's frank, is daddy in?"

Felicia rushed to the door gladly and opened the door. "Daddy is not in but you can sit and wait for him sir."

Frank "Oh thanks my daughter, I have to leave now, my regards to mommy and tell daddy I checked on him alright."

Felicia " Alright sir, good bye."

She closed the door and rushed to Helen. " Mom, it's daddy Frank, he came to check on dad, he sent regards to you."

Helen " Alright remember to tell your dad once he is back from work."

It was 2:45pm. George, a giant looking man with a pointed face and grey mustache in his middle 60's stood knocking on the door.

Jethro, a young man of 19 years of age, he had tiny eyes and fat lips with growing bears on his face. He also has a tiny scar just above his left eyelid. He answered " Yeah who is there?

George " It's me, come and open the door."

Jethro "Oh dad."

He went straight to the door and opened it. "Welcome dad, how was the office today?"

George stepping in " I'm fine and the office was fine son. Moving toward his room.

Felicia rushed him. "Daddy, daddy welcome home."

George " Wait, wait don't stain my clothes you just deep your hand in your lunch let me change my wears, let me wear light clothes you will hug me later ok."

Felicia " Daddy Frank checked on you some hours back."

George " Alright I will call him later. Where is your mommy?"

Felicia " She is in her room having a nap, should I wake her up?"

George " No, let her be, just tell Jethro to get my lunch." He walked to the sitting room and sat.

Jethro brought the lunch.

George " Get me my phone from the room."

Jethro went to the room and brought the phone. George collected the phone and dialed Franks phone number.

Frank "Hello, I checked on you some hours back."

George " Yeah I'm back home now, can you just come over now?"

Frank "Ok, I will be right there now."

George "Alright."

Minutes later, Frank knocking on the door. George stood and went to open the door.

George " Welcome Frank, please come in let's have a lunch.

Frank " Alright, where's my funny daughter?"

George "Oh Feli, she must have been watching cartoon in her room." They both laughed and sat.

George " Hey Jethro, more juice please." They began eating their lunch. Jethro brought more juice. After the lunch, they continued chatting and cracking jokes for hours then later Frank left for home.

It was 5:00pm. Oliver, a tall looking young man aged 23, he looks handsome with a tiny pink lips and bold eyes, he has a pointed nose that makes him appear more gentle than his natural self. He stood by the door knocking.

Ava, an 18 years old girl with an average height, a round face and fat lips answered "Yeah, who is at the door?"

Oliver " It's me and Logan, open the door." Ava hasted and opened the door, hugged both Oliver and Logan.

Oliver " Your welcome hug is not important Ava, get us our meal now." He smiled walking in and threw his notebook on the cushion while Logan followed behind.

Ava " Hey, I finished your lunch, only Logan has lunch in this house today." She joked. Oliver turned and looked at her, " Good joke Ava." He smiled again.

Logan, a 23 years old young man with giant statue, a pointed nose, growing bears and side box, answered. " If I have a lunch Oliver also has a lunch Ava. Where is daddy Frank?"

Ava "He is having a nap, not too long he came back from daddy George."

Alice came out the room, " Hello welcome my sons. How was the school today?"

Logan "Fine mom."

Ava brought the lunch and kept on the table.

Alice " Please sit down and have your lunch dears."

Oliver staring at Ava " Good girl."

After the meal, Logan went home showered and had a nap.

It was 9:45am. Oliver knocking on the door.

Felicia " Yoh, who is at the door?"

Oliver " Its Oliver, is Logan home? Come and open the door feli."

Felicia rushed and opened the door, once he stepped in she hugged him.

Oliver "Wow, how are you doing today? Ain't you going to school today?"

Felicia " Yap, no school today, we are on break now."

Oliver " I see the excitement in you. Is he home?"

Felicia "Yes let me call him." She walked towards Logan's room shouting his name.

Logan " Yeah, Feli what's up?"

Felicia "Oliver is here, its time for school."

Logan met Oliver in the sitting room, they had a handshake

Oliver " Ready?"

Logan "Yeah ready."

They both walked out of the compound.

Logan "Shit, it's sunny out here, let me get my sunglasses quick.

Oliver "please fast man, it's getting late."

Logan " Will be back in a second." He rushed towards home. Seconds later, he came back wearing his sunglasses, they walked to the road, stopped a taxi and boarded then off they went to school. As they arrived school, they moved to their respective departments. Logan entered the class and sat on the desk, he removed the sunglasses from his face and kept on the desk and paid attention to the lecturer. When the lecture was over, he walked out and dialed Oliver's number.

Oliver " Yeah what's up, are you done?"

Logan " Yap, where are you now?"

Oliver " In the hall, we are almost through, just come over."

Logan started walking to meet Oliver but when he remembered he left his sunglasses on the desk, he turned and went back to the class to grab it but as he reached the class, he couldn't find it there. He asked a lady nearby if she met any sunglasses as she sat there. The lady replied " No but I heard someone asking for the owner of a sunglasses."

Logan " please can you identify the person?" The lady pointed at other the lady.

Logan "Oh thanks." He walked to meet the lady.

CHAPTER TWO

LOGAN, JANE AND OLIVER

Logan met Jane "Hello, I was directed to you, I am the owner of the sunglasses you picked on the desk, I heard that you were asking for the owner."

Jane, a 19 years old beautiful, slim tall lady with blue eye balls, pointed nose and reddish lips replied " Alright, lucky you, I want to go in few minutes, had you delayed coming back minutes more, you wouldn't have met me here." She smiled and handed over the sunglasses to him while staring straight at his eyes.

Logan "Oh thanks, am a lucky type, always lucky." He smiled and collected the glasses.

Jane " Yeah I see, it's good to be a friend of a lucky type, let's keep in touch." She gave an admiring smile.

Logan "Yap it's good to be a friend of kind people, take my number."

Jane " How am I kind?"

Logan " Yes you are, sure, I see it." They exchange contacts and Logan left to meet Oliver. When he met Oliver, they stopped a taxi and left for home.

The next day 7:20am, Oliver dressed up and rushed to school to attend a class as Logan wasn't having any lecture to attend on the day. After the class, he went to a cafeteria to take his breakfast, he ordered for coffee fried plantain and eggs with slices of bread, as soon as he was served he started eating with rush, he was very hungry. Then here came Jane, she placed her order and sat waiting. Oliver observed her staring at him, he suddenly slowed down his eating. Jane noticed that and smiled. She was served and soon she started eating. From time to time she exchanged glances with Oliver. Oliver was almost done with his breakfast, he took the last sip of his coffee when it hooked him in the throat and he started coughing. Jane observed. "Oh sorry, easy."

Oliver raised his head to looked at Jane " Thanks dear." He said uneasily and coughing continued. Jane stood and rushed to meet Oliver, she screamed at the waiters please bring water for him now. Someone rushed with a bottle of water, Jane collected and opened it, she then gave it to Oliver and told him to drink the water. Oliver collected the bottle and drank the water, immediately he began to recover. Jane " Are you alright now?"

Oliver " Yeah I feel much relieved now." Jane went back to her breakfast. Oliver stood and went straight to pay bills for both him and Jane, after the payment, he went and met Jane.

Oliver "Thanks for your kind assistance dear."

Jane "Oh it's alright, hope you are fine now."

Oliver " Yeah, am alright now. Wish to meet you again, love to have your contact to say hi from time to time."

Jane " Oh thanks, don't mind, we can say hi anytime we meet yoh, no need to call ok."

Oliver "Cant let you go without giving me your phone number, can't let a beautiful kind creature go without getting connected, you are not the type to be missed by opportunity, there are a lot of good things about you, just tell me your phone number now please."

Jane smiled " Let me have your phone." She extended her hand. Oliver quickly handed his phone to her, she collected it and dialed her number, Oliver collected the phone back.

Oliver "Am Oliver Frank." He extended a handshake.

Jane smiled "Am Jane David." They had a hand shake.

Oliver "You don't need to pay your bills I have done that for you."

Jane "Oh, thanks, I appreciate."

Oliver " Thanks too."

Jane "Alright bye."

Oliver "Good bye." Oliver left.

It was 11:00am. Logan dialed Jane's number, it rang but no answer. Few minutes later, Jane called back and Logan answered the call.

Jane "Hello, good morning."

Logan "Good morning Jane, how are you doing today?"

Jane "I'm doing great, how are you too?"

Logan "I'm fine dear, I just call to say hi, hope you had a nice day the other day."

Jane "Yeah I'm always having a nice day."

Logan " Are you off lectures today?"

Jane " hmmm not really, we gonna have it later."

Logan "Alright enjoy your time before then."

Jane "Enjoy yourself too."

Logan "Bye."

Jane " Good bye."

Jane was really interested in the gentle nature of Logan and she was looking forward to having him as her new boyfriend. Though she didn't know what exactly Logan felt about her. She believed that it was just a matter of little time for her to detect his position.

It was 8:30pm, Oliver dialed Jane's number, it rang but there wasn't response. Thirty minutes later he called again and this time she answered.

Jane " Hello, who's on the line?"

Oliver " It's Oliver the guy you met at the cafeteria in the morning."

Jane " Alright, what's up?"

Oliver "I'm cool yoh, I thought you got my number saved with my name."

Jane "Oh, no, I forgot to do that."

Oliver "How are you doing Jane?"

Jane " Yeah I'm fine."

Oliver " Thanks once again for that day."

Jane " Oh come on, you don't have to keep thanking me everyday, it's just a normal thing."

Oliver "Yeah I understand but to me it's a special thing from you."

Jane " How?"

Oliver " I mean I see you and everything you do as special."

Jane " Wow you may see it that way but you don't really have to."

Oliver " I wish you can grant me 30 minutes of your time to see you tomorrow at the cafeteria."

Jane " My time, why do you want to see me?"

Oliver " There are words that I wanna tell you which are beyond expressing on phone, we need to meet."

Jane " I don't think I have enough time to meet you there tomorrow but I will check my schedules and get back to you soon."

Oliver " Alright I will be anxiously waiting."

Jane ended the call.

Jane in the real sense had enough time to attend Oliver's invitation but she didn't want to meet him so she deliberately ignored him without calling him back as she said. Oliver on the other hand kept waiting for her call but was left disappointed.

The next day around 8:00am, Oliver dialed Jane's number and she answered.

Jane " Hello."

Oliver " Good morning Jane."

Jane " Good morning."

Oliver " I have been expecting your call yesterday but you didn't."

Jane " Oh, I was carried away by other things don't mind me. Anyway I don't think I have time to meet with you today, maybe someday I will call you if time permits alright."

Oliver "Alright but I will keep reminding you cause it seems you are a busy type so you need a reminder." He smiled.

Jane " You may be right that I'm a busy time but I could be much idle sometimes. Anyway, you are free to remind me as you wish."

Oliver " Yeah I will remind you all the time Jane." He joked and smiled again.

Jane " No, not all the time Oliver, not all time. She frowned and ended the call.

Oliver was not happy with her last response but deep inside him, he was already in love with Jane so he had no choice but to be patient for now.

It was 2:00pm, Ava dialed Jethro's number, his phone rang and Jethro answered.

Jethro " Hello dear."

Ava " What's up boy, where are you now?"

Jethro "I'm at home, is everything cool?"

Ava " Yeah everything cool just come over now."

Jethro " I know Daddy Frank is still at the office now but what about mummy Alice?"

Ava " She has been working hard since morning and now she is into deep sleep."

Jethro " Wow it's great but how about Oliver?"

Ava " Why all these questions? You know if we ain't gonna be safe I won't invite you yoh. Just come over now don't make it late yoh."

Jethro quickly rushed to meet Ava, as he arrived the entrance door he gently sneaked in and went direct to Ava's room. He met her wearing a sleeping gown and not wearing pants and bra. Immediately he stepped in she grabbed him and engaged him in a hot romance.

Jethro whispered" Let's not forget to luck the door."

Ava whispered back "Yeah you are right."

She stepped and lucked the door from inside. She then began to off her clothes while Jethro watched. His penis was already very hard, she moved closer and began to help Jethro off his trousers while he was pulling his shirt. He threw the shirt on the flow and gently pushed Ava flat on the bed, he dipped his middle finger into her vagina and she made a slight scream of pleasure.

Jethro whispered " So you are already wet for me."

Ava impatiently whispered back " Just fuck me now I have been horny since morning. Jethro splitted her legs wide open and introduced his hard-standing penis into Ava's vagina. She gave a sound that tells he touched the right place. They did it for like 15 minutes and it was over and both were satisfied. Jethro sneaked out and went back home while Ava went straight to the bathroom and took shower.

It was 8:30pm, Jane dialed Logan's number and when it rang, Logan answered.

Logan " Hello Jane."

Jane " How are you doing today?"

Logan " I'm doing fine, and you?"

Jane " Fine, it's been quiet sometime now that I heard from you."

Logan " Yeah, I have been around, I'm just calm you know…."

Jane "Yeah aren't you going out to cinema, watching sports, always home?"

Logan " I do watch sports but not often. I love being at home reading novels, that's my hobby."

Jane " Wow it's nice, you got a good hobby boy."

Logan " What's your hobby Jane?" He smiled.

Jane " I got so many hobbies like playing chase, cards, chatting and rough playing." She giggled.

Logan giggled too. " I love rough play too but with someone strong I mean a male."

Jane " Not all men are strong, are you with me?"

Logan " How do you know Jane?"

Jane " Because I used to smack men down years back." She joked.

Logan giggled " Not real men Jane."

Jane " What determines real men?"

Logan " Physical, emotional and mental strengths Jane."

Jane laughed " That's not what determines real men alright. A real man is a man with a male sexual organ that knows how to use it very well and then with the qualities you mentioned above."

Logan " Wow I see, this conversation is getting interesting and I'm getting educated."

Jane "Oh really, I can teach you more. Where are you now Logan?"

Logan " At home."

Jane " Meet me in school, would you mind that?"

Logan "Yeah, it's my pleasure Jane. I will be there soon."

Logan took a brief shower, dressed up and rushed down the road to board a taxi.

Jane was aware that the lecturer had postponed the lecture, so she then walked up and sat at student garden to wait for Logan. When Logan arrived school, he called Jane to know her location, when she told him, he went to met her. As he arrived, he met her there sitting with her legs crossed and staring at him with confidence. As he came very close, he smiled and extend a hand shake but instead Jane stood up and gave him a warm hug. This sent a message to him and as well gave him confidence too. They both exchanged greetings and sat facing each other.

Logan “Wow you’re looking smarter this morning.”

Jane “Oh thanks dear.”

Logan “ How about the class?”

Jane “ He ain’t coming but I have to stay cause I’m gonna have another one soon.”

Logan “ Alright, how are you doing Jane.” He admired.

Jane “ I’m cool yoh, would you mind a juice?”

Logan “ Why, sure.”

Jane ordered for two bottles of juicy drinks.”

Logan’s phone rang it was Oliver and he answered.

Logan “ What’s up boy?”

Oliver “ Cool yoh, where are you?”

Logan “ At school.”

Oliver “ Don’t what?”

Logan “ I checked on a new friend.”

Oliver “ Alright I will be there right away.”

Logan “ Meet us at the student’s garden.”

Oliver “Alright then.” He ended the call.

CHAPTER THREE

OLIVER TURNS RIVAL

They were served juicy drinks and they began sipping and having interesting conversations. Some minutes later Oliver approached the garden as he drew closer, he recognized both Jane and Logan but both Jane and Logan were off minded and busy with their conversation so none of them sighted him. Oliver was shocked at seeing Jane with Logan, and even though Logan referred to Jane as an ordinary female friend but Oliver was intelligent enough to detect that such friendship can easily turn into romantic relationship. He hid behind a car parked some distance away from them, he had no idea of what to do at first, he stood watching how Logan cracked jokes while Jane broke into laughter. He suddenly grew jealous of everything going on there, he wished he was the one sitting with Jane right there but unfortunately Jane didn't seem to give him opportunity to express himself as he was supposed to. He thought he didn't have to go there because Jane would definitely recognize him and on his own part the feelings of annoyance and jealousy would surely show at least on his face and by so doing, Logan would understand everything, so he decided to visit a male friend so he quickly left. When he left the school premises, he called Logan and Logan answered.

Logan " What's popping it's taking too long. Where are you now?

Oliver " Sorry boy I had an important call and my attention is demanded so I have to be there."

Logan " Hope it's alright."

Oliver " Yeah it's alright, thanks. He ended the call.

It was time for the lecture and both Jane and Logan said goodbye to each other and departed to their different destinations.

It was 5:30pm, Henry 20, a tall handsome man with a face that resembled that of fake reverend fathers dialed Ava's number, it rang but there wasn't answer. He had been dating Ava for almost a year now, he loved her so much that he so much relied on her, he didn't friend other girls because he believed in faithfulness, he had been attempting to have romance with Ava for almost a year now but she kept resisting, he knew that she loved him so much but her excuse for the resistance was always the same, that she wanted to remain decent till she gets to 20 years of age. Henry loved her so much and he was such a patient and easy-going young man, so he didn't bother much except on rear occasions that he temporarily lost control when tempted by her beautiful facial looks and sexy body. Ava on the other hand didn't really mean to be decent, deep inside her, she didn't trust Henry because she believed that once she allowed him to have sex with her he would dump her and commit to other ladies. She knew how ladies admired Henry because of his handsome looks. She knew that Henry loved her for real but she was afraid of loosing him to other ladies after giving him what he had been thirsty of for long, she always loved his company because he was presentable as a boyfriend anywhere at all times. One thing she so much loved about him was his natural gentility and he loved buying her gifts. Whenever she remembered all the nice things he did for her, most of the time she felt guilty when she denied him sex and have it freely with Jethro, her neighbor. When this thoughts came up on her mind, she always claimed right in her mind that she couldn't resist having sex whenever she was horny.

Few minutes later she came out of the bathroom and checked her phone, she saw Henry's missed call, she called him back. Henry answered.

Henry " Hello Ava."

Ava "Hello, sorry for the delay, I was in the bathroom dear."

Henry "Yeah I guessed so, I stood for over 10 minutes now."

Ava " Oh I'm so sorry about that, I will be out now. She quickly dressed up and met him outside the compound. As she approached closer, she gave him a gentle warm hug. Henry was pleased to see her dress so beautifully, he was also pleased with such a gentle warm hug. He began to flatter her while she was smiling and looking straight into his eye balls. He held her arm and off they went to attend a basketball match.

It was 8:30pm, Oliver dialed Jane's number, it rang and she answered.

Jane " Hello, good day."

Oliver " Hi Jane, how are you doing today?"

Jane " I'm fine and you?"

Oliver " I'm good dear, it's quite a while now that we talked on phone, I just want to say hi, I believe you're alright."

Jane " Yap, I'm alright and thanks for the call."

Oliver " Yoh one more thing, I want to remind you of our appointment Jane."

Jane "mmmh, I thinks we can meet tomorrow. Just call me anytime tomorrow alright."

Oliver " Alright, I will be glad to meet you Jane."

Jane "Alright till then." She ended the call.

Few minutes later she called Logan and he answered.

Logan " Hello Jane."

Jane " Hi Logan, how are you doing?"

Logan " I'm very fine Jane hope you're doing great."

Jane " I am but only if you care to call me as I do Logan."

Logan " Baby you are right, I needed to have called to Know how good your day was like, I mean I need to call and say hi. He smiled.

Jane " Oh sure, so you know the right thing to do right."

Logan "Oh real, pardon please, you know these hobbies of mine get me carried away that I even attend classes lately at times."

Jane "You got to change Logan, you know there are a lot of things that are important so you don't play with. She smiled.

Logan " Including you Jane, you're important too, may be you will influence me to change and take important things serious someday."

Jane " Yoh sure, I wish I could, would you like that?"

Logan " I will love that Jane, what a positive impact, I will be glad Jane." He smiled.

Jane " You will change Logan." She smiled too.

Logan "Alright, I look forward to meeting you again."

Jane " Alright, bye." She ended the call.

It was around 4:30pm, Oliver dressed cutely, he wore expensive perfume and expensive wrist watch, he took a look at himself in the mirror and confirmed he was looking good, next, he opened his drawer and picked some pieces of 100 notes of US dollars, he arranged them in his wallet and pocketed the wallet, then he grabbed his phone from his bed and dialed Jane's number and she answered.

Jane "Hello."

Oliver " Good evening Jane and how was your day?"

Jane " My day is great, how are you doing?"

Oliver " I'm fine, what's up Jane, can we meet now?"

Jane "Mmmmh, I think so but where do you want us to meet?"

Oliver " Let's meet at the Mcsmart center, King Francisco street."

Jane "Alright I will be there in a while." She ended the call.

She got into the bathroom and took a brief shower, came out and dressed up nicely, she took a brief look at herself in the mirror and she was impressed by her looks. She walked out of the compound to the road. She stood on the road for few minutes and finally got a taxi, she boarded in and off they went. As she arrived there she met him already waiting for her. As she approached, stood from where he was sitting he walked towards her and attempted to hug her but she declined and said " it's not everyone I hug, please stop it." He face frowned.

Oliver " Oh come on girl, this is just normal Jane."

Jane " Normal to you but as for me, I carefully select those that can hug me." She said with pride.

Oliver " Wonderful, it's alright let's have a sit."

They both walked and sat facing each other with a table in between. Oliver looked straight into Jane's eye balls in admiration while he was smiling. "You're such a sweet girl that every man will love to have."

Jane " Not everyone Oliver, another man like you may not admire anything about me."

Oliver " Why do you think so Jane?" He smiled staring steadily at her. He turned, looked at a young man close by and ordered him to bring drinks. He turned looked at Jane and asked what kind would you like?"

Jane "Oh no, please don't bother to buy for me I don't need anything."

Oliver " Come on you need to take something dear, please just feel free."

Jane " I'm free boy, I'm just alright."

They continued having conversations but the conversations was a kind of boring because Jane wasn't picking interest at all. Oliver then excused Jane, went in and bought a lot of snacks and drinks for Jane, he got everything packaged and presented it to Jane as a gift. Jane received it and thanked Oliver. Few seconds later Jane got a call and she answered.

Jane " Hello dear."

Logan "Hi Jane where are you?"

Jane " I'm not at home, anything Logan?"

Logan " mmh not much, I thought you are in school, I'm done with my class for today. I just wanna say hi."

Jane " Wow you have started to improve boy." She smiled.

Logan " Yeah sure."

Jane " Yeah sure, just wait for me there am gonna meet you now." She ends the call.

She looked at Oliver and said " I gotta go right now."

Oliver frowned his face but remain speechless. Jane stood up picked the package and started walking away.

Oliver stood up, " ok let me see you off."

Jane " No, no don't worry I will be fine, thanks." She even walked faster. Oliver stayed back having a terrible feelings of jealousy and anger. He felt more irritated whenever he remembers how she walked away from him because of Logan, to him that was unacceptable. He sat there for a long time trying to figure out a way to tackle this annoying challenge. He couldn't end at any reasonable idea but vow not to give up on Jane.

It was quarter pass 8pm, Logan knocked on the door to the entrance of Frank's compound. Ava sitting on a cushion in the sitting room. " Yeah who's there."

Logan " It's Logan yoh, is Oliver home?"

Ava "Just come in Logan."

Logan stepped in and saw Ava watching film on a laptop so he asked again, "Is he home?"

Ava " He is supposed to be unless if he went to see his girlfriend since you are still afraid to talk to any girl Logan." She joked.

Logan smiled " I'm not afraid any longer Ava, I have got one now."

Ava paused the film and stood up, "This is unbelievable, who is she and when did you suddenly develop confidence to talk to ladies now, Logan when have you grown up?" She joked and broke into laughter.

Logan "You so much love jokes Ava, was I a kid before?" He smiled.

Ava " Someone that can't toast a lady is a kid."

Logan " If that is the case then there are many kids around." He smiled.

Ava " You are the only male kid in your home because your younger brother Jethro is a man for a long time now."

Logan " Ava you are talkative I'm not here for you, continue watching your film and enjoy yourself dear." He giggled.

Ava laughed " I know you wouldn't like to argue much cause you can't defend yourself here."

Logan " I have heard you but at least I'm not single now Ava." He smiled and walked fast to check Oliver in his room.

As he stepped in, he met Oliver playing games on his phone, as Oliver saw him he paused the game. " What's up boy."

Logan " Yeah I'm cool, I got a good news for you."

Oliver adjusted his sitting position " What's good boy?"

Logan sat close to Oliver " There's this girl named Jane, we met as friends but her body language is telling me that she is picking interest in me. She was the friend I was with the other day I asked you to meet us in the student's garden. Oliver adjusted again while starring at Logan with deep but hidden envy in him.

Logan continued. " She always talks about romantic relationship, rough play and she loves talking dirty whenever we communicate. We met today and now she is challenging me for sex next week if I think I'm a man. She said I was only lucky that she is in her menstrual circle today she could have proved to me that she is a real woman. But we really had a good romance today."

Oliver " Wow, wow you really had a nice day today but where did you do it?"

Logan " Jane has money, she Lodged a room for us and paid the bills."

Oliver " This is crazy, she really loves you but don't allow her to turn you into a sex toy alright."

Logan "Are you sure?" Panicking.

Oliver "Yeah sure boy, you gotta reserve yourself."

Logan " Alright brother, I will play the card smartly, I will keep you update. But right now I have to go home I have a test to write first thing to do in school tomorrow morning."

Oliver " Best of luck Logan."

Logan " Thanks yoh."

They had a hand shake and said goodnight to each other then Logan left. Oliver was deeply hurt by this ugly news, he was imagining the girl that he so much admires was openly rejecting him because of Logan which he thought was inferior to him in terms of physical looks and social experiences. To him, this is an unacceptable insult upon his personality. What pained him most is his inability to quit the relationship, he thought it seems the more Jane rejects him the more he develops stronger feelings of uncontrollably affection for her. He knew he was simply infatuated over Jane. His heart continued to beat faster and soon he developed headache which denied him a comfortable sleep in that night.

It was Tuesday morning around 8:45am, Frank knocking at the entrance door to George's compound.

Helen " Who's at the door please?"

Frank " It's Frank."

Helen " Frank come in please the door is not locked."

Frank opened the door and stepped in.

Helen " Good morning sir."

Frank " Morning, how are doing?"

Helen " I'm doing great, how is my friend Alice?"

Frank " She is doing well too, is George home?"

Helen "Yes but he is taking his bath now, he will soon be out. Have a sit sir."

Frank " Oh thanks. "

He sat in the sitting room and focused on the television. Few minutes later George came and met Frank. He extended a handshake to Frank.

George " Good morning Frank." Frank shook him while smiling. "Good morning George, I'm lucky you haven't gone to work yet I was trying to rush."

George " Yeah, there isn't much to do at the office that's why I don't bother going early all these days however, am set to leave now."

Frank " Well I have an important request George, I just hope am going to be granted."

George adjusted his position and leaned forward " What's it Frank?"

Frank cleared his voice " I need you to lend me some money to invest in a transportation business, they remit certain amount as profit six times in a year. The profit is enough to recover my total capital within a short time. I see this as an opportunity and soon they will close the sell of shares to interested persons."

George " How much do you want to lend Frank?"

Frank cleared his voice again " A hundred thousand dollars and we are going to make it official and I will sign the collection of the money and also state the date for the refund sir."

George smiled" It's alright we have all the time in the world to put it in written that's not a problem. I trust you Frank."

Frank gave a satisfactory smile and said " I'm ever grateful George, once I get the money and invested, I will carefully study the business and I will invite you to also join."

George " It's alright Frank, am wishing you the best. So when I'm back from office I will call you."

Both Frank and George stood up and started walking towards the exit.

George opened the driver's door of his car then turned and asked. " One more thing, do you want it in cash or bank transfer?"

Frank " I prefer it in cash, yeah cash."

George " Alright then." He nodded his head.

They both had a handshake, said bye to each other and departed to their desired destinations.

It was 6:00pm, George called Frank on phone and Frank immediately answered the call.

Frank " Hello George, are you back home?"

George " Yeah I'm back now, can you please come over?"

Frank " I will be there right away."

Few minutes later, Frank stepped into George's compound.

George " Welcome Frank, have a sit please."

Jethro also sitting in the sitting room watching an interesting program on the television. He turned, looked at Frank, " Welcome daddy Frank."

Frank " Thanks my son, how are you doing today?"

Jethro "I'm fine sir." He focused back on the program in the television.

George " Get me my office bag Jethro, it's on my bed in the room."

Jethro " Alright dad. He quickly went to the room and brought the bag.

George collected the bag and opened it while Jethro stood and watched George brought out a bunch of new hundred dollar notes. He zipped up the bag and handed it back to Jethro, Jethro collected the bag and stood still waiting for order. George turned and faced Frank. " This is a hundred thousand dollars

Frank, you can go ahead and invest as you wish and I can give you even more time to pay the money back as you proposed. I trust you won't disappoint me Frank."

Frank quickly grabbed the money and said " I will never disappoint you Frank, you are more than a friend, more than a good neighbor you are equal to a caring brother now." He smiled.

George " We are brothers Frank." He turned and asked Jethro to take the bag back to the room.

Frank " When do we put this in written George?"

George " Oh come on Frank, we have plenty of times to do that, I'm just coming back, I gotta rest and don't worry about that we can do it any day."

Frank "Alright George I have to leave now, please have a good rest. Thanks brother."

George " Alright then, thanks too."

Frank left for home. George went back to his room and had a good rest.

It was 8:15pm, Logan knocked on the door to the entrance of Frank's compound. Alice was sitting on a chair in the sitting room. " Come in the door isn't locked." Logan opened the door and stepped in.

Alice " Oh Logan my son, how have you been doing?"

Logan " I'm fine ma, how is daddy?"

Alice " Daddy is fine."

Logan " Hope Oliver is at home."

Alice "Check him in I think he is around."

Logan " Alright ma." He gently walked in and met Oliver in his room.

Oliver " Hey what's up boy, I missed your call and I ain't got airtime to call back."

Logan " You turn broke boy, it's a pity." He joked.

Oliver " I got money in the bank but I'm just barely broke."

Logan " Hey stop pretending, I know you are broke boy. You got money in the bank and you can't recharge your line?" He joked.

Oliver confessed " Yoh I'm broke and what is my offense for being broke?" He smiled.

Logan "Now you're talking." He brought out two pieces of dollar notes from his pocket and threw them to Oliver. "Take this and buy airtime boy."

Oliver grabbed the money quick. " Thanks boy, so what's popping man?"

Logan sat close to Oliver. " Man, Jane is driving me crazy. We had another round of crazy romance today, it was really hot."

Oliver frowned his face, "This Jane is distracting your focus on your studies, don't let this continue."

Logan " But I wrote my test quite good today, she ain't distracting me."

Oliver frowned again " Look boy I ain't gonna be part of this, am a changed man now, you see you got to avoid all this shit for now!!"

Logan " Did I hear you call yourself a changed man now?" This is unbelievable, you can't turn into a saint overnight, you are addicted to women Oliver." He giggled.

Oliver " I mean what I said Logan, at least I will stay well focused for now but by the time I graduate then I can resume my lifestyle fully. How do you see that?"

Logan " Yeah it's a nice idea go on boy but as for me I won't miss the opportunity before me I gotta sex Jane." He smiled.

This sounds unbearable to Oliver, the expression on his face started showing his intense level of jealousy, he felt like dragging Logan on the neck to suffocation there and then.

Oliver " I can't stop you from doing what you are pleased to do but remember we are in our final year, a critical level of our program so it's left for you to choose between success and failure."

Logan leaned back with his face facing the ceilings while he was thoughtful. Oliver was carefully starring at him disdainfully. Oliver thought what could Jane have seen in Logan that makes her love him so much? Oliver believed he is far better than Logan in all aspects, he believed he looks far more handsome than Logan, he believed he is taller and has more interactive ability when it comes to relating with ladies. He strongly believed that he deserves Jane as a girlfriend and sex mate more than Logan. He wished Jane had taken her time to realize his handsomeness, smartness, extravagance and other physical and attitudinal advantages he has over Logan and made him her choice not Logan. But unfortunately, Jane had not realized anything, then something is wrong he concluded.

Logan " I thought of what you said boy you are really on point but I have to make love to Jane like twice or thrice then I will quit." He smiled.

Oliver " I'm out of this Logan." He snarled. He stood and went straight to his toilet, as he grabbed the handle of the toilet door, he turned and looked at Logan, "Can we meet later please? I'm gonna be busy now."

Logan " Why, sure." He stood up and left for home.

Two days later, Jane was now through with her menses, she took her bath and came out of the bath room wearing towel over her chest. She sat on the bed having an irresistible feelings of sexual urge. Her father, David was a business tycoon, very religious, disciplined and strict in attitude and he excessively provided her with all that she needed. As a student, she had over a hundred thousand dollars in her bank account with nothing to use the money to purchase, she was willing to take care of any man that sincerely loved her and could give her a very good sex. All she wanted was a good sex anytime she needed it. Jane had been used to regular sex since three years ago and now for months she had not been touched by any man. Bruce, her former boyfriend had graduated from the school and went back to Canada where he lived with his parents, they only talked on phone once in a while, he was carried away by his new job and new girlfriend. During his reign in relationship with Jane, it was really fun, they had sex on a daily basis, he was very good in bed, sometimes he could sex Jane about four or five times a day. Bruce had the sexual strength to last for over forty-five minutes on top of Jane per a round of sex and he had a very strong and lasting erection. Whenever Jane had the thoughts of their romantic and sexual affairs, she usually found her pants already wet. she had been searching for the right guy to be quenching her sexual urge for months now and she believed Logan is the very right guy for the job. She didn't like having sex or even inviting men into her apartment because her father paid her surprised visits several times unexpectedly. She knew he could come at anytime he wished and once he caught her having sex with anyone, she would be toughly penalized by him, he would also not have confidence in her again. To avoid unnecessary drama, she felt safer to do her dirty things in the hotel room.

She looked at the watch on the wall and it was 4:30pm. This is the right time for the job, she thought. She grabbed her phone and dialed Logan's number, when his phone rang, Logan answered the call. " Hello Jane."

Jane " Hi Logan, how are you doing today?"

Logan " I'm doing great Jane and you?"

Jane " I'm fine boy, where are you now Logan?"

Logan " I'm at home now."

Jane " Alright, I got something special for you. Let's meet at smarter guest hotels as usual." She smiled.

Logan " Wow, are you sure?" He smiled.

Jane " Yeah, sure it's gonna be hot boy, you can do whatever you wanna do today."

Logan " Are you real, is the flow over?"

Jane " Yeah I'm real, it's over now and today is gonna be rough." She smiled.

Logan giggled " I see, let's meet then."

Jane " Alright then." She ended the call.

Jane dressed up attractively and glanced at herself in the mirror, she opened her drawer and grabbed some money and pocketed it, then picked up her phone and inserted it inside her other pocket and walked out. As she reached the main road, she boarded a taxi and off they went. When she arrived, she checked in a hotel room and ordered for snacks, soft drinks and other eateries. She peeped into the bathroom room and she saw that it was neat and beautiful, she sat on the bed and felt so eager to see the arrival of Logan. She brought out her phone from her pocket and called Logan, it rang and Logan answered. " Hello Jane, are you right there?"

Jane " Yeah, I'm right there now, where are you?"

Logan " I'm on my way already, I will be with you in a minute."

Jane " Alright come straight to room 09."

Logan " Alright Jane." He ended the call.

As he arrived the room, he knocked on the door. Jane stood and stepped over to the door and asked, Yeah Logan?"

Logan " Yap it's Logan."

She quickly opened the door, as he stepped in, she looked at him, her eyes full of admiration. She locked the door and gently hug him from the back. He turned and grabbed her waist, her hands over his shoulders and she began kissing him. Immediately his penis was erected she went on her knees and zipped down his trousers and grabbed his erected penis and dipped it into her mouth, he screamed for pleasure with his hands squeezing her hair. At a point he couldn't withstand the pleasure, he screamed "wait, wait Jane." She stopped while impatiently looking at him.

Logan " This is crazy yoh, let me off my shoes Jane."

Jane helped him to off his shoes while he was sitting on the bed. He pulled his shirt and she helped him pulled out his trousers. Logan was naked now with his pinkish head-penis standing erect, Jane was already wet, she quickly got herself naked and mounted herself on top of Logan, she personally introduced his penis into her vagina and the game was on, the round lasted for like 20 minutes before it was over. They were both satisfied and weak, Jane reached out to her phone, "Hey boy, I will love to remember you on this special day." She smiled and began snapping them while they were both naked. Logan wasn't comfortable with that. "Make sure you keep the pictures highly confidential." He said worriedly.

Jane smiled " Yeah sure, trust me, my phone is on a finger print security."

Logan " That's cool yoh, let me snap you alone, I trust your styles girl." He smiled.

Jane passed the phone to him, he collected and snapped her some pictures. She collected the phone and watched the pictures. She giggled " You are a bad boy Logan, this is really cute." She said nastily.

Logan " Let me see the picture."

Jane passed the phone to him, he collected the phone and looked in with amusement. " Wow this is cute, I bet this can arouse me anytime I take a look again. "Please send the pictures to my phone."

Jane sent the pictures to Logan's phone and they both wore their under wears, then Jane brought the eateries, they fed on having fun, an hour later then Jane started again, she proposed they should bath together in the bathroom, they went in then Jane initiated a rough play and that led to another round of sex, this time Jane gave him a doggy style. It was really hot. It was a very sweet and memorable day for the both of them. After the sex, they had shower, then chatted for sometime, checked out of the hotel room and left for home.

CHAPTER FOUR

THE DEATH OF LOGAN

It was 5:45pm Jethro sneaked into George's room while George was away to spend his time with his friend Frank. Helen was very busy in the kitchen preparing dinner for them. As he stepped into the room he went straight to his daddy's wardrobe and quickly opened his daddy's bag and took some money, he closed the bag and gently walked out. Immediately he stepped out of the compound he dialed his friend's number Carlos, when it rang Carlos answered, " Hello J.

Jethro " What's up boy?"

Carlos " I'm cool yoh, what's popping?"

Jethro " Nothing much, where are you?"

Carlos " In the street."

Jethro " Let's meet at our joint now."

Carlos " Alright, I will be there."

Few minutes later they both met at the joint, there they met Chris, Alex and Don playing cards. A half bottle of whisky standing by the side of Don on a dwarf center table, Alex remained focused on the game while Chris flicked off cigarettes ashes on the little tray beside him.

Jethro " Hey guys." They all turned to look at both Jethro and Carlos.

Chris "What's up men."

Carlos " Yeah what's good?"

Don played his last card, turned to look at Carlos, "Nothing is good boys except this half bottle of whisky." Chris played a card, dragged hard on his cigarette. "And this last stick of cigarettes." He said as smoke came out of his mouth.

Jethro " I need a rolled stick of weed urgently." He demanded.

Alex " And you can't have any here J, we urge for it too but we are all broke to have one here."

Jethro " This is serious, we got to smoke well today guys." He said with pride on his face.

Don took a long sip of his whisky, turned to look at Jethro," Yeah I see it, it's like you are heavy in the pocket."

Jethro " Yeah I got some bucks, hey Alex please drop the card and let's get our brains charged yoh."

Alex " How do you want it to be?"

Chris passed the cigarettes to Jethro, Jethro dragged it hungrily. Carlos demanded the bottle of whisky from Don, Don took one more sip and passed it to Carlos. Jethro blew out smoke from his mouth and said " Let's be fast on this Alex, you and Chris will go down the streets to get us some rolled sticks of weed and cigarettes, Carlos will take care for our drinks." He brought out some money and handed it over to Alex and Carlos, they grabbed the money and off they went. Don adjusted his position staring at Jethro. " It's pretty nice with you this evening, I'm proud of you." He gave a nasty smile. Jethro dragged the cigarettes and passed it over to Don. He sat facing Don arranging the cards. Few minutes later, Chris and Alex returned. Jethro turned to look at them "Everything cool?"

Alex "Yap, everything cool." He dropped some weeds and packs of cigarettes on the center table.

Chris "Where is Carlos, isn't he back yet?"

Don "He will be with us soon."

Jethro picked a rolled stick of weed, lit it and dragged it hard. Alex watched Jethro as he also reach to picked one rolled stick. "Pass me the lighter J." Jethro threw the lighter to Alex and blew out smoke from his mouth. "I can't do without this shit called weed, now I feel am alive." He said as he critically watched the burning stick of weed in-between his fingers. Carlos stepped in. "Wow so the shit is already on." He said cheerfully.

Chris turned to look at him. " The shit is on but it can't be good enough without these bottles in your hands Carlos." Carlos took one from the sac and placed the sac on the center table. Don stared at the bottles, "These are expensive j, it's a great evening then."

Chris reached for a bottle, opened it, took a long sip and said " We could have been dull here without a stick of cigarettes if not for you Jethro. He smiled

Don flicked off ashes from his cigarette, " Money is good, I can do anything to get rich."

Jethro " You said anything?"

Don " Yeah I mean anything either legal or illegal."

Alex "I'm with you Don, I can do any damn thing to get rich too you know...."

Carlos took a long sip, " Money brings the fun all the time, it's important, it doesn't matter how you get it."

Chris "You are right Carlos, I don't give a damn about how I get money, being rich is worth taking risks."

Don grabbed a bottle from the sac on the table and opened it, he took a sip and said "One day we will be rich either legally or illegally that's what I believe."

Chris " Sure boy even if it requires robbing a bank, I won't give a damn, I hate being broke." He snarled and took another sip.

Jethro gently dragging his weed while staring at Chris with his left eye half closed avoiding smoke into it. " You are right boy I admire your courage, you are a man."

Alex " Robbing a bank requires enough guns and that is where the problem is."

Don " Guns may not even be the problem but the perfect plan to rob a bank is the primary problem."

Carlos " Alright boys if we can brainstorm we can do it and be rich once and for all."

Jethro " Let's first get a target bank and study it very well."

Don " You are on point Jethro."

They continued to drink and smoke having funs until it was over and they all left for their various homes.

It was 11:15am, Oliver dialed Jane's number, it rang and she answered, "Hello"

Oliver " Hi Jane, how are you doing?"

Jane " I'm good"

Oliver " It's quite a while we met Jane, I just remember you and I feel to tell you that I care."

Jane " Oh thanks boy."

Oliver " I will love it if you allow me to pay you a visit."

Jane " No, I don't have much strength now, I have been sick for a while now, I can't attend to you now."

Oliver " Oh, serious?"

Jane " Yeah serious, I'm sick."

Oliver sympathized " I can't wait to see you Jane, I feel sorry for you please allow me to come and have a glance of you please, I won't stay long Jane." He said softly.

Jane " Alright, you can come 8pm."

Oliver " Alright Jane, I will be there by then."

It was 1:30pm, Logan called Oliver on phone, Oliver was reluctant to answer the call but he finally decided to answer the call. "Hello Logan what's up."

Logan " Yeah cool boy, where are you now?"

Oliver " I'm at home now, anything special?"

Logan in excitement " Yap very special, I will be there in a second." He rushed and met Oliver sitting on the bed, Logan smiled "Let me show you something." He searched the pictures in his phone and threw it to Oliver. " Flip and watch the pictures boy, I have done it." He said with pride.

Oliver grabbed the phone and saw picture of Jane naked on bed with Logan wearing boxers only. He looked at her breast standing erect with small reddish nipples, he raised his head and glanced at Logan with great anger in his eyes and then flipped the next picture and saw Jane resting her head on Logan's chest, her eyes half closed and her lips pinkish, he truly admired her looks but he hated her for what she was doing at that moment. He raised his head again to look at Logan that was still standing in his front. "But this is crazy Logan." He said with anger in his voice. Logan giggled staring at Oliver. Oliver flipped the next picture and saw Jane alone stylishly laying naked on the bed, he looked at her sexy hips and her half shaved pubic hair and that nearly got him aroused. He raised his head to look at Logan again. "This is nothing but bullshit Logan take this phone I'm not interested in watching this irresponsible pictures, I think I told you that am a changed person for now!" He shouted with anger in his voice. Logan extended his hand and collected back his phone. " Yeah now I see how serious you are about the change you said. I don't like your mood but I caused it, anyway I'm sorry but I gotta go now." He gently walked out. Oliver watched Logan as he walked, he couldn't bear this emotional pain, he had to find a way to stop these threats to his peace of mind he thought. He had vowed to do anything that will guarantee his emotional stability back, it doesn't matter what that thing could be, he couldn't just allow any body to exposed him to heart attack which could lead to hid early grave. The pain of the indirect insults was too severe to bear he concluded.

When it was 6:45pm, Oliver took a brief shower, dressed up and walked out. He stopped a taxi and boarded in. He stopped at a provision store and bought some juicy drinks, snacks and special greeting card with an inscription "GET WELL NOW MY ANGEL CAUSE WHEN YOU ARE SICK, I ALSO FEEL THE SAME INSIDE ME. IM TOO ATTACHED TO YOU GIRL." The card looked expensive and stylishly unique.

He paid the bills and quickly walked out, there was a chemist store nearby, he also stopped there to buy a rat poison and a syringe as he bought the items he then turned walking towards the exit of the store he met Edward a course mate he knew in the school with a lady walking into the store, they met along the corridor of the store and had a handshake.

Oliver "Edward what's up" He smiled.

Edward " Cool Oliver, what's popping?"

Oliver "Nothing much boy, I just got some items and I gotto rush somewhere now."

Edward " Yeah I got it right you got bought some condoms and you wanna rush to meet her right." He joked.

Oliver smiled " No Ed, it's not what you think this time. I guess it's you that find someone and now you're itching to get the rubbers to start the fun." They both broke into laughter and departed.

When he came out of the store, he found an isolated place nearby and brought out all the items in the sac, he used the syringe to draw out the poison into the syringe and injected the poison into the juicy drinks, he then used a sticker to carefully cover the tiny hole. It looked perfect and nobody could detect it, he studied it well and saw that it was okay, he gave a nasty smile, threw away the poison bottle and the syringe then he put back the remaining items into the sac and moved on quickly.

It was 7:30pm when he arrived the junction to the compound where Jane lived, it was already dark because the sky was cloudy. As he approached closer, he saw Jane and Logan under a beam of light from an electric bulb, he immediately stopped and made some few steps to hide behind a car that was parked closed by, he sighted as Jane hugged Logan, Logan held her hand and kissed her hardel. She gave a beautiful smile and kissed him on the forehead. She hugged him again and they said farewell to each other. Oliver felt irritated by seeing them doing that, he whispered to himself. " This is the last time you will do this Jane, you can't kill me with unbearable pains Jane." When Logan approached, Oliver further ducked and watched him passed by. After Logan had gone and Jane went into the compound, Oliver started his way again towards the compound. He gently knocked on the door and Jane came over and opened it, as she saw him, she gave a half smile. " Oliver, you're welcome, come in please."

Oliver " Thanks dear." He watched her tempting buttocks as she led him in.

Jane " Have a sit please." She pointed at a plastic chair.

Oliver " Oh thanks, I see that you feel much better now."

Jane sat on a chair close to him. "Not really, am just trying to be strong."

Oliver " Sorry, I believe you will be alright soon."

Jane " Yap hopefully."

Oliver " I just feel like I got to see you today, you know I care about you Jane." His face broke into an innocent smile.

Jane "Oh thanks for the care boy." She said faintly.

Oliver opened the sac and started bringing all the things he bought, he gave her the card. " This is for you Jane." He smiled again.

Jane smiled and collected the card, she carefully stared at the card reading the inscription. "This is nice but are you sure you're too attached to me? I don't think so boy." She giggled.

Oliver stared at her as she spoke, having it in his mind that she would already be dead by this time tomorrow. He smiled. " It could be so Jane, I also got all these for you Jane." He handed everything to her. Jane collected and thanked him.

Oliver " Alright I got to go now before it's late, please be punctual on your drugs ok."

Jane "Alright, thanks and good night."

Oliver " Alright then." He walked out.

It was 9:00am, Jane called Logan and he answered. "Hello Jane."

Jane "Logan how are you doing?"

Logan " I'm cool yoh, hope you are stronger now."

Jane " Strong enough to wrestle you boy." She joked.

Logan smiled. " Yeah I see, that's great Jane."

Jane " Please do you mind to come over now?"

Logan " Why sure, am not busy."

Jane "Please come over am lonely, I need someone to talk to."

Logan " It's my pleasure to be with you dear, I will be right there."

Jane " Alright see you soon."

When Logan arrived he met Jane a bit weaker than she sounded on the phone. She was happy to see him, they had a cheerful conversation for a long while she then went to the refrigerator, picked up the juicy drinks that Oliver bought for her, repacked them in the sac and brought them to Logan and said, " This is for you Logan you may take it home dear." She smiled.

Logan sitting on a chair collected the sac and looked in, he raised his head looking at Jane. " Oh come on Jane, it's you that deserve this from me."

Jane " Don't worry Logan, please take it home it's for you boy, I love you."

Logan gave Jane and admiring look, he smiled beautifully and replied, " Love you too."

After sometime Logan left for home. When he arrived home he met Ava and Jethro playing card in the room. Ava turned to look at him, "Mr. Lover man." She joked.

Logan " You can say that again because am at the peak of the game now."

Ava " Wow I see, what do you get in the nylon?"

Logan " Some drinks, she bought it for me."

Ava " This girl is serious, what's her name?"

Logan " She is Jane by name."

Ava " Jane, what a beautiful name. I love the name, now I trust you are a man. Congrats, Jane loves you Logan. Enjoy yourself boy."

Logan " Thanks Ava." He walked to his room.

It was 10:30am, Oliver knocking on the door.

Felicia " Yeah who's at the door?"

Oliver " It's Oliver, come over and open the door Felicia."

Felicia rushed and opened the door. As he stepped in Felicia hugged him. " Good morning pal."

Oliver " How are doing my dear?"

Felicia " I'm fine as you can see."

Oliver " Wow that's beautiful dear. Where's Logan?"

Felicia " He is in his room."

Oliver " Alright let me see him." He walked towards Logan's room. He knocked and knocked without any response.

Helen came out of her room to check the person knocking. Oliver turned to look at her, "Good morning ma." He said uneasily.

Helen " Good morning my son, I believe you're doing great today."

Oliver " Yeah I'm great ma, I have been knocking and no response at all, is he out."

Helen " I believe he is in but maybe still deeply in sleep, call him on phone."

Oliver brought out his phone and called Logan, he heard the phone ringing. " He is in then" He said with relief. He opened the door and stepped in. He saw Logan lying on the floor with his mouth halfway opened, foams coming out from the mouth, his eyes turned reddish widely open and motionless. He also seemed to be lifeless. Oliver got frightened by the horror looks of Logan in such condition and screamed out, the sound immediately sermoned the attention of all the available members of the house because Jethro wasn't at home at the time. They met Logan dying, they quickly searched around and saw some used containers of juicy drinks. Oliver looked carefully and noticed that it was the drinks that he bought for Jane and injected poison into he wondered how it got to Logan's hands, he concluded that she gave it to Logan. He felt terrified because he knew that Logan would not make it alive again. He personally knew that there would be serious problem ahead. George picked his phone and called the ambulance, he described his home address and asked them to rush to save life. Helen packed all the items and put them in the sac. George took Logan's phone and pocketed it. Oliver was squatting close to Logan's chest carefully studying his breath. Oliver's heart was pounding terribly, his forehead continuously generating sweats.

When the ambulance arrived Helen handed over all the containers of the juicy drinks to the doctors for laboratory investigation. They received them, then placed Logan on the bed and rushed him to the hospital.

Oliver " I pray he will be fine, daddy George I got to drop this lecture notebook home and tell my dad what's happening here."

George "We are going to the hospital now, tell Frank to me us there." He said uneasily.

Oliver " Sure dad, we will meet you there now." He said, his voice trembling.

Felicia was already crying bitterly while tears rolled down the chins of Helen, George was emotionally unstable. They all rushed into the car, George drove out fast and off they went to the hospital. As they arrived the hospital they waited anxiously to know what the problem was, few minutes later a female doctor came out and announced that Logan was dead and they found out that he drank poison and the poison was contained in the drinks he took last night. George and his family were all panicked, speechless and lost idea of what to do, their hearts pounding. A gentle looking male doctor approached them, "Sorry for the lost of your son Mr. George, I advise you should involve the relevant authority for the investigation of the death of your son sir."

TO BE CONTINUED IN THE VOLUME 2.

WATCH OUT!

www.ingramcontent.com/pod-product-compliance
Lightning Source LLC
LaVergne TN
LVHW020538160826
845677LV00015B/4134

* 9 7 9 8 8 4 8 2 9 4 0 0 2 *